I0692611

Henry Thornton Craven

Milky White

A Domestic Drama in Two Acts

Henry Thornton Craven

Milky White
A Domestic Drama in Two Acts

ISBN/EAN: 9783337342203

Printed in Europe, USA, Canada, Australia, Japan

Cover: Foto ©Andreas Hilbeck / pixelio.de

More available books at **www.hansebooks.com**

MILKY WHITE

A DOMESTIC DRAMA IN TWO ACTS

BY

H. T. CRAVEN

New American Edition, Correctly Reprinted from the Original Authorized Acting Edition, with the Original Casts of the Characters, Synopsis of Incidents, Time of Representation, Description of the Costumes, Scene and Property Plots, Diagrams of the Stage Settings, Sides of Entrance and Exit, Relative Positions of the Performers, Explanation of the Stage Directions, etc., and all of the Stage Business.

Copyright, 1889, by Harold Roorbach.

NEW YORK
HAROLD ROORBACH
PUBLISHER

MILKY WHITE.

CAST OF CHARACTERS.

	Prince of Wales Theatre, Liverpool, June 20th, 1864.	Olympic Theatre, New York, Nov. 21st, 1864.
DANIEL WHITE (unpopularly known as "Milky White," a Cowkeeper)	Mr. H. T. Craven.	Mr. W. Holston.
DICK DUGS (a Cow Boy)	Mr. James Stoyle.	Mr. C. T. Parsloe, Jr.
ARCHIBALD GOOD (a Veterinary Surgeon)	Mr. S. Bancroft.	Mr. T. B. Berry.
RUDE BOY	Master Cheeky.	
MRS. SADDRIP (Neighbor of White, and Proprietress of a Baby Linen Emporium)	Miss S. Larkin.	Mrs. G. H. Gilbert.
ANNIE WHITE (Daughter of White)	Mrs. H. T. Craven.	Miss Louisa Myers.

One Night is Supposed to Elapse between the Acts.

TIME OF REPRESENTATION.—ONE HOUR AND THREE QUARTERS.

SYNOPSIS OF INCIDENTS.

DANIEL WHITE, derisively called "Milky White," and hated by his neighbors with whom he is at constant war, is a sour tempered, deaf old dairyman, idolizing his daughter ANNIE, the only person for whom he has a kind word. DICK DUGS, his assistant, and ARCHIBALD GOOD (*alias* SMITH), a young veterinary surgeon ambitious of becoming a great physician, are both in love with ANNIE who returns the latter's affection. GOOD's father, having been forestalled thirty years before, in a love affair, by his partner, had revenged himself upon his false friend by disappearing from home and causing it to be supposed that he was dead. He had afterward married in another part of the country and subsequently died, leaving to his son a legacy with which the latter had purchased the reversion of four thousand pounds, payable at the death of a

SCENE PLOT.

ACT I. White's parlor, set in 3 G., backed with dairy and cow-yard in 4 G. The dairy is a paved and whitewashed chamber railed off from the parlor, and occupies one half the width of the stage between the third and fourth grooves R., it has a rough latched door on the L. side, which opens to the cow-yard. Distributed on the walls and floor of this dairy are a churn, yokes, and a number of milk cans of all descriptions. The parlor occupying the stage as far back as the third grooves is neatly papered and comfortably though humbly furnished, with the exception of a piano placed down R. A door (supposed to open to the street) R, 3 E., with a practicable bolt or lock on its inner side. Another door, on which hangs a large slate, L. 2 E. Fireplace and mantel-shelf at L, 3 E. A green wooden railing or fence running from R. 3 E., to C., of flat, with gate mid-way, separates the dairy from the parlor. In the half flat, L. C. is an open window, with curtains, through which the cow-yard is seen. Easy chair near window; table L. C. with chairs on each side of it. On the walls hang an old-fashioned clock, picture of a cow, and a whip. Door mat at door. R. 3 E. Carpet down.

ACT II.—White's bedroom, in 3 G., backed with interior (corridor) backing in 4 G. Door R. C. in flat. Door R. 2 E. Fireplace and mantel-shelf L. 2 E. Curtained bed (made up) up C., against flat, with its head R. Chest at foot of bed. Chair between head of bed and door, R. C.; another chair near the head of bed. Easy chair down L. Small round table near fire place. Toilet table down R., on which are a mirror, comb and brush. Portrait of Annie hanging against wall, over bed. Rug or piece of carpet down.

STAGE DIRECTIONS.

The player is supposed to face the audience. R. means right; L., left; C., centre; R. C., right of centre; L. C., left of centre; D. F., door in the flat or scene running across the back of the stage; R. F., right side of the flat; L. F., left side of the flat; R. D., right door; L. D., left door; I E., first entrance; 2 E., second entrance; U. E., upper entrance; I, 2 or 3 G., first, second or third grooves; UP STAGE, toward the back; DOWN STAGE, toward the footlights.

R.   R. C.   C.   L. C.   L.

NOTE.—The text of this play is correctly reprinted from the original authorized acting edition, without change. The introductory matter has been carefully prepared by an expert, and is the only part of this book protected by copyright.

MILKY WHITE.

ACT I.

Scene.—*Daniel White's Parlor and Dairy.*

DICK (*a cowboy*) *passes the window, from* L. U. E., *and* **enters** *at the door,* L., *in dairy, carrying heavy milk cans with a yoke, which he leaves at back, and comes through gate of rails ; wipes his feet on the rug and enters the parlor, crossing to slate, which hangs on the door,* L. 2 E.

Dick. (*as he writes on slate with a lump of chalk*) There ! I've pumped the cows and milked the pump ; now to chalk it up and send it out. What a persevering chap I am ! hooked three new customers yesterday in the place o' one as hooked it the day afore ; our walk will soon run through the whole parish, and all along o' me ; but my master—Milky White, as the boys call him, don't 'preciate me properly. Why ain't my wages riz ? Why don't he give me a share in the business, if it comes to that ? Why, if I was to go and leave him, he'd lose more than half his customers ; for though he's my master, there never was a mortal so mortally disliked—he hasn't a blessed friend—always going to law with somebody or another. " Milky White's a brute ! " " Milky White's a onfeeling monster ! " " I should like to see Milky White ruined and in the workus ! " them's the pleasant little observations as I'm obligated for to listen to from the neighbors ; and why do I stay to be blowed up and worked thirteen hours a day ? Why don't I strike ? he can but knock me down for striking ; ah, here comes my answer.

Enter ANNIE, *door* L. 2 E.

Annie. (*crossing to* C.) Now Dick, look alive or you'll catch it. Where's father ?

Dick. (L.) In the cow yard with that 'ere swell young cow-doctor—Smith. That young chap's got talent, mind ye ; he's saved Bessy, the short-horn ; she's getting round again, and the gov'nor's as pleased as Punch ; he seems to take to the young surgin as you fetched, uncommon, and that's saying something ; for he's the most passionate, short temperdest brute as——

Annie. (*seated* R. *of table and working*) Don't you dare to say such things to me, Dick ; he's a good father, and never denies me anything.

Dick. (L. *of table*) No, Annie, 'cos you're his strong weakness ; it's my opinion he doesn't care a ha'porth of sour milk for any one else in the world, and I'm getting into the same way myself. Do you care for *me ?*

Annie. Care for you ? of course I do ; ain't I always kind to you Dick ?

Dick. You always looks out that I have wittles enough, that I *will* say for you ; but my heart wants feeding as well as my stomach, and something come over me, Annie, as undermindges all my appetite : the pudding as you make sticks in my throat, and without making any fuss about it, I feel that I'm quietly walking into my tomb.

Annie. Oh, Dick, keep yourself up, or what's to become of us all ?

Dick. Keep myself up ! I can't keep *myself* up ; it depends upon you whether I don't flop down altogether. You wouldn't like to see the red cows feeding on the green grass as grows over my grave, would you ?

Annie. Gracious ! no, Dick, for I'm sure they wouldn't yield on that ; besides, they wouldn't be allowed to graze in the churchyard.

Dick. (*pathetically*) But don't let 'em drive 'em away, Annie. I couldn't rest happy if I didn't know as the beings I milked when I was alive, was feeding on me when I was diseased. (*sheds tears*)

Annie. But you're robust enough ; you're not going to die.

Dick. You wouldn't like to see it, would you ? Then have I your leave to speak to Milky ?

Annie. Of course, Dick ; if there's anything on your mind, have it out with father, like a man.

Dick. I'll beard the lion in his cow-house ; I'll make him understand, deaf as he is. (*going up to dairy, and taking his yoke and cans*) Bless you, Annie, you've made the cream of hope rise to my top ; now I can cheerfully serve out the skim.

Exit *at door*, R. 3 E., *and is heard without, calling* " Me-a-ow ! "

Annie. What can he have to say to father ? Poor boy, I dare say he wants a rise of wages—ten shillings a week isn't much—he's worth more.

Archibald *appears at the window, from* L. U E.

Arch. Gentle Annie ; here I am again, you see. (*disappears, and* **enters** *parlor through the dairy, coming down,* L.)
Annie. You seem to take great interest in our cows.
Arch. Cows ! vaccine idea. No, I've an aspiration above that, and mean to go in for a degree in the regular college of surgeons ; I'm only two and twenty, and not going to be a vet. all my life. I shall adopt a specialty, that's the way to rise ; and I've been reading up the pathognomonicks of the human ear —for it's my opinion there's a good deal to be done in cases of deafness which has never yet been thought of.
Annie. My poor father is dreadfully deaf, I wish you could do something for him.
Arch. I *have* diagnosed his case——
Annie. Dognosed it ? What's that ?
Arch. Thought about it.
Annie. Is that all ?
Arch. It's simple enough. (*sitting on table*) You see, his deafness was produced by a violent blow on the left mastoid process ; now the membrana tympani at the extremity of the meatus oratorius being perforated, cannot communicate its vibrations to the nervous fasciculi, and——
Annie. Are you talking to me ?
Arch. Yes.
Annie. Then surely English would be more musical.
Arch. It would ; his drum's broken, and the organ being destroyed, a trumpet is useless.
Annie. But can you assist him ? that's the question.
Arch. We'll see ; I've invented an artificial gutta-percha tympanum, and I'll try it.
Annie. I think it's partly the deafness which makes him so irritable.
Arch. Irritable ! there's no telling how to have him ; but with all his faults, there's something in the governor's character I like.
Annie. Ah, I'm so pleased to hear you say so, for everybody seems to have a harsh word for poor father.
Arch. He's so confoundedly fond of going to law ; I believe he has no sympathy but with you and his cows ; but even they, one would think, might give him some milk of human kindness.
Annie. I often fancy there is something on his mind.
Arch. I know what it is.
Annie. You ! and known him but three weeks——
Arch. (*taking chair and sitting* L. *of* ANNIE, *drawing close to her side*) Annie my, girl, tell me a secret, and I'll share mine with you. Do you really and truly love me ?

Annie. Archy, for a sensible young man, what a goose you are.

Arch. True ; you decided my fate last Michaelmas ; in fact, you hinted a week ago, that if I can squeeze out your father's consent, you will become my own little wife. Oh, the delight of having a wife of one's own !

Annie. Yes, I think it's best to have one of one's own ; don't you ?

Arch. Listen to a soporific relation.

Annie. What's that—an intended husband ?

Arch. No, a sleepy story. My father was once treacherously forestalled in a love affair by his partner—rushed far from the scene of his blighted hopes ; and what revenge do you think he took on this false friend ?

Annie. Killed him ?

Arch. No ; he killed himself.

Annie. Then you never had a father ?

Arch. When I say he killed himself, I mean he caused a letter to be written to this false friend, giving an account of his suicide ; don't you see ? That was calculated to produce remorse, which ranks first as a lasting punishment.

Annie. Sometimes I have imagined poor father suffers from something of that kind.

Arch. That was thirty years ago ; time passed, and my inconsolable dad found a wife in Jersey. I was the sole result.

Annie. What's the result ?

Arch. I mean, I was the only child.

Annie. Why didn't you say so ?

Arch. My mother died five, and my father two years ago ; he had educated me for a veterinary surgeon, but all the money he left me was two thousand pounds.

Annie. Why, Archy, you told me you were as poor as a church mouse :—two thousand pounds !

Arch. I haven't a penny of it.

Annie. You wicked spendthrift !

Arch. Speculation. I bought at Garraway's the reversion to four thousand pounds, which I shall come at on the death of a man of sixty.

Annie. Then you are anxiously waiting for the man of sixty to die ?

Arch. Well, not exactly ; though I have heard it is likely to happen very soon. But he's a wicked old fellow, and according to all accounts, the sooner he's gone the better.

Annie. And what will you do when you get the money ?

Arch. Run away with you ; it was my father's last request that I should see you, and if I could love you (which I do— dearly) to complete his revenge by taking from White his only treasure.

Annie. (*dropping her work*) Then my father was——

Arch. The false friend. (*rises*)

Annie. (*rising*) And you think I will break his heart by such a deed ? Never ! Unless he should drive me from him, I will never leave without his consent.

Arch. (L. C.) He casually told me to-day that he'll never consent to your marrying at all.

Annie. (C) Then I must stay with him and be his comfort ; poor man, he has no wife—no other child, and if he thought I did not love him better than all the world, I'm sure he would die.

Arch. And you make such a trifle as that an obstacle to my happiness, after all the trouble I've taken to fall in love—that is, to gain your love ! Didn't I, regardless of expense, secure a lodging in the very house where I found you went to take music lessons ? Haven't I doctored all your father's cows for nothing ? Am I not going to operate upon his ears——

WHITE *appears at the window*, L. C.

White. (*in a blustering voice*) Here ! hi ! hulloa ! you doctor chap, come here ; I want you as a witness. I'll enter an action against the Company !

Arch. (*going up*, L. C., *to window*) What's the matter ?

White. Here's a 'bus scraped the paint off the wheel of my dung cart ! I'll be down upon 'em. (*calling off*, L.) I'll see my solicitor about this ; what's your number ? Take the vagabond's number ! hi ! hulloa ! he's off ! (*disappears*, L. U. E., *and is heard without, calling*) "Stop him ! stop him !"

Arch. (*crossing to* L.) There he goes ; he'd spend twenty pounds in law to recover a sixpence for paint ; ha ! ha ! he *is* a character !

Enter MRS. SADDRIP, *without bonnet, at door*, R. 3 E.

Mrs. S. (*coming down*, R.) Oh, Miss White, will you excuse my speaking before a stranger ; but my heart's full—do you know of this ? (*holding out a copy of a writ*) Here's a writ served on me by your father, because my cat killed three of your young chickens. I couldn't help it ; I offered to pay for them, but he's determined to bring it into Court. To serve an unprotected woman and a next-door neighbor this way is too bad ; he's a wretch !

Annie. No, no, don't say that ; I dare say he didn't understand that you offered to pay, for you know he's so deaf.

Mrs S. Deaf! I wish he were dumb too, for of all the abusive men—— oh, it's dreadful ! but I'm not afraid of him ; I'll give it him !

White. (*re-appearing at window*, L. U. F.) Some rascal has put a dead rat into my water butt ; that's Mother Saddrip's rat,

I know the breed ; she shall pay smartly for it, if she don't, may I——

WHITE **enters** *through the dairy and comes down*, C.

(*seeing* MRS. SADDRIP) Holloa ! ho ! hey ! what are you doing in my parlor ? Who sent for you—what do *you* want ?

Mrs. S. (R.) You know well enough, you wretch !

White. (*as though listening*) What do you say—you're a widow ? I know you are ! poisoned your husband, everybody knows it. I know what *you* are—any one can see what *you* are.

Mrs. S. (R., *to* ANNIE.) Oh, did you ever !——

Annie. (*back*, C.) Never mind, he doesn't mean anything.

White. (C., *to* MRS. SADDRIP, *who holds the writ in her hand.*) You're right, I *am* going to lug you into Court, that's just what I'm going to do.

Mrs. S. No wonder you're hated by everybody ; I wouldn't have the odious character you've got in the neighborhood for all the gold in the mint.

White. That's all soft soap ; I'm *not* a good-hearted man at bottom, as you shall find. Did you put that dead rat into my water butt ?

Mrs. S. I, you wretch ? what a filthy idea, no !

White. Oh, you say you saw Jones do it, did you ? very well, I'll subpœna you, I'll rat you, drat you. (*to* ARCHIBALD *who comes down*, L.) You're witness she says she saw Jones do it.

Arch. (L. *aside*) Bless me, if I don't take care, he'll make me perjure myself before I know what I'm talking about.

White. (C., *to* ARCHIBALD) You're right, those were her very words, (*turning to* MRS. SADDRIP) but I haven't done with you yet, Mother Saddrip.

Arch. (*aside*, L.) Is her name Saddrip ? Now that's very singular.

White. You'll have to bundle out of your house ; I mean to throw a nest of cow-sheds through your wash-house.

Mrs S. A nest of cow-sheds ! why, you're talking like a madman as you are ; I've got a seven years' lease.

White. I've offered to buy the premises of Blotch, if he'll bundle you out.

Mrs. S. But he can't do it !

White. What do you say—" You hope we won't be hard upon you ? " You shall see—you shall see.

Mrs. S. Do you understand this ? (*snaps her fingers under his nose*)

White. Yes, that means impidence ! You mean to say you defy us, eh ? Now, look here, according to your lease you was to paint yourself down every three year—now, to my knowledge, you've been four year in that house, and never even washed

your outside—it's disgraceful ! what must your *inside* be ? The
lease is null and void—*(snapping his fingers under her nose)*
do you understand that, eh ? Besides, I'm not always going to
have your trumpery shop under my nose ; you'll have notice to
quit, to-day.

Mrs. S. You monster ! Mr. Blotch is too much a gentleman to
do such a thing ; I believe it's a wicked fabrication.

White. I can see that woman's kicking up a row—take her
away ; I mustn't have my peaceful home disturbed—take her by
the shoulders and put her out ! (ARCHIBALD *crosses to* MRS.
SADDRIP *and persuades her to go)*

Mrs. S. *(at door,* R. 3 E.) Ugh ! you abominable wretch !

Exit, R. 3. E.

White. Throw something at her ! *(turning to* ANNIE, *who is
back,* C.) Annie, my girl, give us a kiss — why you've only
bussed your old dad once to-day ; you know you haven't, you
puss ! *(kisses her heartily)* There go and buy yourself that smart
little bonnet you took a fancy to. *(gives her money, and she is
going out at door,* R.) Stop ! Stop ! *(she returns)* It was in
Wilson's shop, wasn't it ? (ANNIE *nods)* Ah, I'm going to indict
him for keeping pigeons that pick all the mortar out of my
chimneys ; go to Dabble's, if you pay twice the money. *(crosses
to* L.)

Annie. *(at back,* R., *to* ARCHIBALD) Isn't he a dear old father ?
I wish he could hear ; I think I might persuade him to do many
kind things, if he could only listen to reason.

White. *(turning and seeing* ANNIE *still there)* There, be off
and get it at once, or perhaps I may think twice about it.

Exit ANNIE, R. 3 E., WHITE *crosses to the door which he opens
and looks after her.*

White. Isn't that a girl of girls, eh, Smith ? What do I care
for all the world, while I've got a companion like that ! Look at
her figure going down the road. *(pointing off)* See how she skips
over that puddle ; that's grace after dinner, isn't it ? talk about
your statutes and your busks ; there's the real article. *(comes
down* C., *with* ARCHIBALD) And that girl loves me too—rayther :
she's an affectionate disposition, Smith.

Arch. (L. C.) I know it, old fellow.

White. (R. C.) You've hit it ; as you say—she's not the sort to
marry and desert her old father. And she's accomplished too—
oh, bless you, I've had her taught a little of everything. Have
you heard her sing ?

Arch. Oftener than you think, old boy.

White. Oh, haven't you ? Well, then it would do you good.
D'ye notice that pianny forty ? that was coming out strong, wasn't
it ? *(goes to piano,* R.) Bought it at a sale, for five-and-twenty

pound; and then summonsed the auctioneer for a wrong description in the catalogue—recovered five. (*poking at the keys with his forefinger*) A nice article, eh?

Arch. (C.) *You* are.

White. And she's the nicest girl—ah, within ten miles.

Arch. That she is; there I fall in with you.

White. (*watching his lips*) You don't think so? (*turning from him with contempt*) You're a hass! And for half a farthing I'd give you an exterior view of my premises, only I want you to operate upon my ears before I bundle you out.

Arch. (*aside*) A *fistic* operation would do you good.

White. (*returning to him*) I don't mind telling you in confidence, but if any young fellow—don't care who—should propose to take that girl away from me——

Arch. (*aside*) He's going to offer her to me.

White. I'd fell the fellow like an ox.

Arch. (*aside*) There's a butcher!

White. No, you're wrong there; she won't be left destitute. To be sure, I haven't saved much money—lost so many confounded lawsuits—but I manage to pay up a heavy life insurance —four thousand pound, Smith; that's pretty well thankee, for a cowkeeper, isn't it! Well, that will be hers when I go aloft.

Arch. (*aside*) Or below; a mere matter of conjecture.

White. You're quite right; it's likely to be long before that happens; but look here, *she* doesn't know that I can leave her anything, and I wouldn't have her know it for the world; promise me as a man—I won't say a gentleman,—because you're no gentleman——

Arch. (*aside*) Complimentary!

White. But promise me, as a man, that you'll never mention what I've let slip out unawares; it would break the child's heart to think it possible that I could ever die; she loves me so, bless her! And as to her leaving me, there's one comfort, she couldn't love anybody else, if she tried ever so hard. What did you say— "gammon?" If you say that again, I'll knock you down!

Arch. Then I'll be content with *knowing* it's gammon, you cantankerous old whitewash vendor.

White. That's enough! If you beg my pardon, that's enough; we'll say no more about it. Now, how about my ears—are you going to operate? (ARCHIBALD *nods*) Have you got your chest of tools with you? (ARCHIBALD *nods*) Then go upstairs to my bedroom, and wait till I come to you. (ARCHIBALD *is going*, L. 2 E.) But stop, come here; mind, if you make a mull of it, I'll proceed against you for practising without a deploomy. I fancy I should recover.

Arch. (L.) Grateful rascal! you deserve to recover.

White. (L. C.) But I don't see why you *should* fail, you understand the 'natomy of a beast—why shouldn't you understand mine ?

Arch. My argument exactly.

White. And when you've done it, I'll give you a treat ; you shall hear·my darling little Nan sing ; there, be off and get your lancers ready for action.

Exit ARCHIBALD *at door*, L. 2 E. (*rubbing his hands*) The very idea of getting back my ears fills me with noble emotions. Won't I go into Court and bully Mother Saddrip ! I hate that woman. (*turning up stage*)

Enter DICK DUGS *at door*, R. 3 E., *with pails which he goes into dairy with.*

Holloa, slow coach, and what are you doing out at this time o' the morning ? Put away your pails, you slouching, idle vagabond, and go and put down your milk. There, don't stare, but *do it !*

Dick. (*crossing at back to* L., *and taking up slate*) He seems rayther good tempered to what he is generally. I'm game to put it to him—blest if I ain't.

White. (*sitting* R. *of table, and taking out an old memorandum book and pencil, writing*) And mind you put it down correct to-day ; don't make such curds and whey of it, as you did yesterday, or I'll knock your wurzel-looking head off ! you— you— (DICK, R. C., *thrusts the slate into the hand of* WHITE, *and stands in a triumphant attitude*) What's this ? (*reads*) "I've been and got two new customers—five-pinters a day." Well, mind you keep 'em up to the mark, or I'll get somebody as will. (*giving slate back to* DICK) Go on with your milk list. (DICK *sits and writes* L. *of table.—*WHITE *is turning over the leaves of his memorandum book*) Let's see, (*scratching his head with his pencil*) I've got summonses out against Jackson, and Hoppy Slope, and the tailor in Clip Street ; that's the way to do business, if they dispute your bill, County Court 'em—put 'em to expense. (*turns and sees* DICK *scratching his head*) What are you forking up your litter about, stupid ?

Dick. (*aside*) I wonder if consent is spelt with a C or a K. (*writing*) K-o-n-s-e-n-t ; that looks all right. (*writing*)

White. Don't forget Mother Cox's new-laid eggs. By-the-bye, who supplies her with milk ? My compliments to Mother Cox, and I'm not going to supply new-laid eggs without I have the milk custom—understand that !

Dick. (*writing*) Business is spelt with a z ; that's it—there. (*rises and thrusts the slate under the nose of* WHITE, *who is looking in another direction—*WHITE *is startled—pockets his memorandum book and pencil, and takes the slate*) I've done it ! Lawks what a prosperation I'm in.

White. (*glancing down the slate*) What in the name of the asylum for idiots is all this ? (*reads*) " I love Annie." (WHITE *drops the slate on to his knee and looks round at* DICK *in horror and disgust—*DICK *unconscious of* WHITE'S *action, has his hand to his heart, and shakes his head sentimentally*) Reach me my horsewhip ! (DICK *is going*) Stop a minute. (*takes up the slate and reads again*) "I love Annie ; Annie loves me !" (DICK *pulls up his shirt collar*) Why you—you—you—stop a bit ! (*reads*) " You'd better give your consent to our marriage, and give me a share in the business—say a third."

Dick. (*leaning across the table and grinning*) That's about the size of it.

(WHITE *with deliberation places the slate on the table— rises, and tucks up his cuffs, which latter action causes a change from exultation to terror in* DICK'S *countenance.*)

White. (C.) Why, ye scarecrow—ye scum—ye sack of grains —get out of my sight or I'll flay you. (DICK *retreats round the table as* WHITE *advances*) Take this. (*flinging at* DICK *the jug which was on the table*) and this ! (*kicking him, as he stoops for his pail in the dairy*) And this ! (*taking* DICK *by the scruff of the neck, putting him to the door,* R. U. E., *and kicking him*) There's my answer !

Dick. (*blubbering*) Oh, that's a *final* answer.

Exit *at door,* R. 3 E.

White. A vermin ! My Nan ! Ah ! ah ! That beats cockfighting ! A rascal, to upset my nervous system, just as I'm going to undergo a frightful operation ; but I'll be even with him—I'll strangle him in the cowhouse. And now I'm a little more calm and collected, I'll let young Smith go to work. (*crosses to* C.) My girl and a thing like that—it puts one in mind of the tale of Beauty and the nasty Beast. Exit *at door,* L. 2 E.

Enter ANNIE (*with a smart bonnet on*) *at door,* R. 3 E.

Annie. (*speaking to* DICK, *who is without*) Father is not here ; come in, Dick, and tell me all about it : don't be afraid ; don't cry.

Enter DICK (*blubbering*), *door,* R. 3 E.

Dick. He's wownded my tenderest feelings. Ain't this a free country ? Why am I treated like a nigger ? I asked him a civil question. Why should he pitch the pitcher at me ? I don't mind his tongue, I'm manured to that ; but why should he kick at me when my back was turned ?

Annie. (L. C.) You must have exasperated my father. What question did you ask him?

Dick. What you told me to. (*crosses to* L., *takes slate from table and hands it to* ANNIE) Oh, the inflammation of his top-boots goes right up to my shoulders.

Annie. (*reads*) Did you write this?

Dick. (C.) Without once looking at a dixonary.

Annie. (R. C.) You presuming, bad boy! How dare you·take such a scandalous liberty? What do you mean?

Dick. What, have *you* turned agin me, after the martherdom I've suffered for your sake? That's worse than the kick. Didn't you tell me as you loved me, and I might speak to Milky White?

Annie. Oh, you quite misunderstood me; I never dreamed that you meant that. I said I liked you, and so I do, for we've been companions for a long time. Dick, don't cry; I can't bear to see a boy cry.

Dick. Then you don't think you could larn to love me?

Annie. No, Dick.

Dick. Don't you think there's anything you could take for it?

Annie. I'll be candid with you, Dick; it's best. I love another.

Dick. (*bursts out blubbering*) That's a settler! That kick's in a wital part.

Annie. Now, dear Dick, I'll make a friend of you—you'll keep my secret, I know. (*putting her arm in his*) Let us take a nice romantic walk in the cow-yard, and I'll tell you who it is—he likes *you* uncommonly; I can tell you that for your consolation. (*he goes up,* C.)

Dick. If I run foul of him when I'm armed with my yokes, I'll give *him* consolation.

Annie. Nonsense, you're a good lad, and I'm sure you'll listen to reason. Come, and I'll tell you all about it; you'll sympathize with us, for you've a large heart. (*leading him through the door in the dairy.*)

Dick. (*as they pass the window, going,* L.) Oh, the small of my back. (*they disappear,* L. U. E., *and are heard talking as they go.*)

Enter ARCHIBALD *from door,* L. 2 E., *and crosses to* R.

Arch. (R. C., *with exultation*) That's done! I've introduced my gutta percha tympanum, and I'll stake my reputation that when he removes the bandage to-morrow, he'll hear as distinctly as I do.

Enter WHITE (*with a white bandage round his ears and head*), *from door,* L. 2 E., *and crosses to* ARCHIBALD, C.

White. (*holding up his finger, threateningly*) Now mind, if I don't recover my hearing after all that, I'll haul you up to the

police court, my fine fellow ; you're not going to try your exper-
iments on me for nothing ; I'm not a cow—d'ye hear ? I'm not
a cow !

Arch. More of a mule.

White. Eh ! what did you say ?

Arch. Nothing ! no matter.

White. It sounded like fool.

Arch. (*aside, delighted*) All right ; it's a successful operation !

White. No tricks with me, my lad, I'm just about the wrong
sort of customer. (*suddenly*) I'm not going to pay you a fee you
know, because you've no legal right to do this sort o' thing—
you're an impostor—I suppose you know that—you're a quack !
but I promised you should hear my Nan sing, and I'll keep my
word. Oh, mind you, I'm a man of my word. (*turning up*)
There she is in the cow-yard, talking to that idiot cow-boy.
(*calling out of window*) Here, Nan—hoy ! (*beckons*) Nan,
my pet, come here ! I want you to sing one of your nice little
songs to the cow-doctor. (ARCHIBALD, R., *expresses annoy-
ance*) Lud, if I could hear her sing—only a little bit—ever so
little. (*coming down*, C.) Doctor, may I lift up the bandage and
try ?

Arch. (*shaking his head vehemently*) No, no, there's danger
of otorrhœa setting in.

White. I'm almost certain I heard while I was upstairs. Didn't
you say something about my hump of benevolence ?

Arch. I said it required development.

White. I've got some rare lumps behind the ear. (*taking
ARCHIBALD's hand, and placing it on his own head*) Now
what d'ye call this here one ? Not-a-bad-sortiveness ?

Arch. (*aside*) His combativeness is the size of an apple dumpling.

White. Now, look here ; whatever you do, don't tell my
darling that I've had an operation performed, it would frighten
her to death, she loves me so, bless her ! (ARCHIBALD, R., *shakes
his head*) Mind you don't, or I'll put you forward—I'll knock
you into the middle of next week !

Enter ANNIE *from* L. U. E., *passes the window, and comes
through the dairy.*

Arch. (*aside*) That's all the apple dumpling. (ANNIE *comes
down*, L., *and touches* WHITE *on the shoulder*)

White. (C., *turning to her*) Ah, Nanny, my pet, come
and sing the cow-doctor one of your nice little songs.

Annie, (*nodding*) I'll sing *you* one, father, if you wish it.

White. Yes, sing that, it'll do as well as any——(*her bonnet
catches his eye*) What's this, the new tile ? oh, it's not half
aristrokatic enough for my pet. After you've sung, you must

get it changed for something more stunning. (*crosses to* L.)
I'll give you the mopuses.

Annie. (C., *pointing to* WHITE'S *head*) Father, what have you
been putting that bandage round your head for? you look so
funny. (*pointing*)

White. Eh? Oh, ah! this thingumbob—oh, I'd got a split-
ting headache right through my bump of benevolence, but it's all
right now. Tune up my lass. (ANNIE *sits at the piano,* R.,
ARCHIBALD *leaning over her and adjusting her music.* WHITE
sits L. *of the table, takes out his knife, and trims his nails)*

Arch. (*to* ANNIE) He thinks this is the first time I have heard
you.

Annie. (*seated at piano and looking back at* ARCHIBALD)
You mean it's no treat; but mind, I sing to please father, he's
such a dear father.

Arch. And buys us such dear bonnets.

White. (*aside*) Has she begun, I wonder? (*aloud to* ARCHI-
BALD) It's beautiful, isn't it? (ANNIE *strikes a loud chord.*)
Holloa!

Annie. What's the matter, father?

White. (*aside, scarcely able to conceal his intense delight*)
I heard something! I heard something! I thought the doctor
had sold me—he's healed me! (*as* ANNIE *plays the symphony,
he looks round and watches her*) She's singing now—beautiful!

Annie. (*sings*)

> Whom did I love, when on her breast,
> I hourly sought my infant rest?
> Whom did I trust in ere my tongue
> Could mock the lullaby she sung?
> Whose gentle form, whose watching eye,
> In cradle dream seem'd ever nigh?
> I had not learn'd to know another,
> For then I only loved—my mother!

White. (*speaking during the symphony*) I wish I could hear
her; I've a good mind to lift up the bandage and try, I will too.
(*draws his chair a little more to* R., *and lifts the bandage from
the right ear—his emotions while the second verse is being sung,
show surprise, delight, and extreme affection*)

Annie. (*sings*)

> Whom did I love as time flew on,
> And she was lost—forever gone?
> Whose doting lip was ever near
> To kiss away my orphan tear?
> Whose fond affection taught me then,

With ardor fresh, to love again ?
No stranger lur'd my heart ; but rather
I clung alone to thee—my father !

Arch. Delightful ! the best song I ever heard.

White. (*wiping his eyes,* L. C.) That's beautiful, that is ; that's the sort of music I shall hear when I go aloft. (ARCHIBALD *suddenly perceives that* WHITE *has partially removed the bandage, and runs to him,* C., *to replace it*)

Arch. (*aside to* WHITE) Are you mad ? You'll ruin yourself !

White. (*aside to* ARCHIBALD, *in great excitement*) It's all right, doctor ! I can hear ! I can—(ARCHIBALD *has re-adjusted the bandage*) No, I can't hear now. (*pointing to* ANNIE) Doctor, that makes us quits, does it not ? (ARCHIBALD *nods*) I should think it did, and something over ; you've got something to give *me* now. (*crosses,* L.C., *to* ANNIE, *who is now turning from the piano*) Kiss me, my darling. (*kisses her with great affection*) Now go and get your bonnet changed, my pet ; get one as pretty as yourself, if there is such a bonnet in existence, (*crosses to* L.)

Annie. Oh father ! (*going,* R. 3 E.)

Arch. (*up* C.) Here, I know something of bonnet anatomy ; I'll go with you.

Exit ANNIE, *door* R. 3 E., *followed by* ARCHIBALD.

White. (L., *turning suddenly*) Hi ! hi ! young Smith ; there's no occasion for you to go too ! (*runs up to door*) Hi !—he's gone. (*comes down,* C.) Now that's a young fellow as is likely to rise in his profession ; he's in earnest in what he does ; he'll come to be a great—hum—ah—earist—that's it—*earist;* and he's a what d'ye call it—a phlebotomist—examines people's bumps—says my benevolence wants development. Benevolence !—what is benevolence ?—doing unto others what nobody will do unto you ; but I've got my ears again—ha ! ha ! Milky White's a perfect man once more. Now I can listen to my darling as she sits and reads to me of a winter's evening—now I—I—I *must* try ; I'm so impatient ; I must see if I can still hear. (*removes the bandage —clock without strikes one*) It's all right ; I can hear like one o'clock ; now I shall listen to nothing but pleasant sounds all day long.

A BOY *thrusts his head in at the window,* L. C., *and shouts.*

Yahoo !—hoo ! Milky White,
He'll growl and bite ;
Deaf as a beadle—Milky White !
Ya-hoo !   BOY *disappears,* L. U. E.

White. (*running up to the window*) Hi ! holloa ! what are

those boys doing in my cowyard ? Cut their young legs off with
the cart whip. (*takes the whip, which hangs on the wall, and
throws it out of the window, off,* L. U. E.) I'll " Milky White"
'em. That's Mother Saddrip's boy ; I know the breed. (MRS.
SADDRIP *speaks without,* R. U. E.) Oh ! here she is ! Now for
any quantity of soft soap ; now she'll try to wheedle me over. (*sits
L, of table*) I'll pretend not to hear her blarney ; I'll gammon
deafness this time.

Enter MRS. SADDRIP *at door,* R. U. E.—*she looks round, and out
of the window.*

Mrs. S. (*at back, to* WHITE *who is seated,* L.) Where's your
daughter, you wretch ? It's no use trying to make such an old
adder as you understand.

White. (*aside*) That woman has evidently taken a degree in
the College of Billingsgate. (*aloud to her, and waving his hand*)
I've got nothing at all to say to you, ma'am. (*aside*) I'll aggra-
vate her by being dreadfully cool.

Mrs. S. (*coming down,* C.) But I've something to say to you,
you bad man !

White. (*aside*) A cowcumber's a fool to me.

Mrs. S. I've just had a notice from Blotch ; you're trying to
ruin a poor, unprotected woman, but a judgment will come on
you for your wickedness.

White. (*aside, chuckling*) She's going mad at my being so
deliciously cool.

Mrs. S. The only being you care for in the world is your
daughter ; she'll be taken away from you, and then you'll hang
yourself ; that's my prophecies !

White. (*jumping up, furiously*) Get out !

BOY *re-appears at the window, points and sings.*

Boy. Milky White, he'll growl and bite——

White. Get out ! (*flinging his hat at the boy, who disappears instantly*)

Mrs. S. (*up,* R.) Folks say your wife never loved you, and
your daughter will be glad enough when you're dead, I dare
say.

White. Vicious cat ; get out ! (*pointing to the door*)

Mrs. S. Do you really hear what I say ? You'll die like a dog
—deserted by everybody.

White. Get out !   **Exit** MRS. SADDRIP, *at door,* R. 3 E.

White. (*coming down,* C.) Isn't it a scandal to a great country
like this, that there's no law to hang a woman at once for saying
such a thing as that ? Why didn't she say it an hour ago, when
I couldn't hear her ? Not that I doubt my child—my darling,
bless her—no ! but the very idea of such a thing makes one's

hair stand on one's end. (DICK *passes the window from* L. *to* R.) Who sent for you ? How dare you show your ugly nose here again ?

DICK *timidly* enters *through dairy.*

There—get to your work (*pointing to the slate, which is on the table*) A double share of work is the share in the business I'll give *you* my lad. (*sits* R. *of table*)

Dick. (*coming* L. *of the table, and surlily taking up the slate*) There'll be a jollification the day as you kicks the bucket. (WHITE, *who is about to blow his nose, stops, and looks at* DICK *aghast*) I'll come the double shuffle on that there occasion.

White. (*aside*) There's a scoundrel for you ! He thinks I can't hear, (*aloud to* DICK) I'll lower your wages my fine fellow; any ass can do *your* work.

Dick. Then do it yourself ! (WHITE *leans back and gapes at* DICK *in astonishment*) But you can't live forever, that's one comfort.

White. (*aside*) Going to murder me ! the murderous rascal ! the—the—

Enter ANNIE, *at door,* R. 3 E., *with a fresh bonnet on ; she runs to* WHITE, C.

Ah, that's something like, that is ! (*rises*) Take it off, my pet, and let's feel the weight on it : (*holds it up admiringly*) That'll take the shine out of the cow-faced girls of Stubbs's, over the way. Put it on again, darling ! By the bye, I mean to indict Stubbs for throwing oystershells into the thoroughfare—confound the fellow, he eats oysters three times a day ; I'll jist look over the Act and see what I can do with him. (*crossing to* L.) I don't believe that, legally, a man *can* eat oysters three times a day. Stand out of the way ! (*pushes* DICK *roughly, who retreats to* R. C.)   Exit WHITE, *through door,* L. 2. E.

Annie. (*crossing and sitting* L. *of table, holding up the bonnet*) Dick, don't you think I can do without this bow ?

Dick. (*sitting* R. *of table*) It seems you can do without this here beau. Don't talk to me about your gimcracks ; I've done with the good things of this world : I'd put 'em all down if I had my way. (*writing on slate*) Half a pint of cream for Mrs. Gollop.

Annie. (*altering the bow on the bonnet*) Nonsense, Dick ; haven't I told you, in confidence, all about Archy ? You're not like the dog in the manger !

Dick. But I don't see as *t'other* dog has much of a chance ; Milky will never consent.

Annie. I don't know that: If Archy should succeed in restoring his hearing, that would be the time to mention the subject, and, as I told you, Archy will have about four thousand pounds, when a certain old gentleman dies, he bought what they call a reversion.

Enter WHITE *from door*, L. 2. F., *turning over the leaves of a pamphlet—goes back to window.*

White. *(as he goes up)* Now, to see what the Act of Parliament says about oyster-shells. *(sits in arm chair by the window, his back being towards* ANNIE *and* DICK)

Dick. *(writing on the slate)* " Three pints of skim at Slopers." Well, go on, Annie ; tell me all about it. Old Milky can't hear us, that's one comfort.

White. *(aside—wheeling the chair round)* Oh, can't he ! What's going on ?

Dick. You think as there's nothing to baulk the marriage ?

Annie. No, for we love each other dearly.

White. *(aside)* What ? what ?—she loves him ! *(pointing to* DICK)

Dick. *(as he writes)* How much money do you say you'll have, when the old fellow dies ?

Annie. Four thousand pounds ;—think of *that*, Dick.

White. *(aside, aghast)* Ah !

Dick. Did young doctor Smith tell you that ?

Annie. Yes ; not long ago, and he says the old man can't live long.

White. *(aside—dropping the pamphlet)* The traitor !

Dick. Then it amounts to this, you wish the old codger was dead ?

Annie. Well, people say it will be a good job when he's gone for he's a wicked old fellow, and does nothing but mischief. It's wrong to wish for anybody's death, but you can't expect *me* to have any love for the old man, can you ?

White. *(gasps)* Oh ! *(sinks back in his chair)*

Annie. *(holding up the bonnet)* D'ye see what effect that's had ? Now, I'll go to the glass and put it on, and I'll try on my new mantle with it. *(Runs off at door*, L. 1 E.

Dick. *(writing)* " Ducks eggs "——

(WHITE, *livid with passion, rushes forward and seizes* DICK *by the throat)*

Dick. *(choking)* Mur-der !

White. *(swinging him round to* C., *back)* Wretch ! Villainous wretch ! leave my house—my door, never—never enter again, or as sure as this hand can grasp a poker, I'll brain you !—out ! out ! *(thrusts* DICK *out at door*, R. 3 E.) Here, here ! your hire—your wages—take it, serpent ! *(flings money out at door; as he does so.)*

Enter ARCHIBALD, *door* R. 3 E.

Arch. (*advancing a step or two from the door*) Hey-day ; here's a rumpus—what's wrong now ? Who's a serpent ?

White. (*up*, C.) You, base betrayer, you !—Never dare to enter my house again, you double-faced hypocrite ; you have betrayed me—my daughter—you it was who poured the poison into her ear.

Arch. (*aside*) Has she then already disclosed our hopes ?

White. You can't deny it—out of my house !

Arch. Undoubtedly, sir, since you addressed me thus. I confess that I was unable to refrain from disclosing to your daughter——

White. Paltry babbler—out of my house !

Arch. At least I have done you no injury—you owe your hearing to me.

White. A curse ! Would that I had remained in my happy deafness—out of my house !

Arch. Madman, adieu forever !

Exit *at door* R. 3 E.—WHITE *rushes up to the door*, R. *and is about to fasten it.*

Enter ANNIE, L. 2 E. *with bonnet and mantle on.*

Annie. (L. C., *without looking towards* WHITE) Dear father, what are you in such a passion about ? How do you like me in my new bonnet and mantle ? (*arranging dress.*)

White. (*rushing down to her*, L. C.) Snake ! ask the gaping world how it likes them ; go out now and ask it ; show it a monster ! a girl monster ! out of my house forever !

Annie. (*falling on her knees*) Dear father——

White. Go, or I'll curse you—you, whom I doted on—you, the only living creature I ever loved, whom I lived for, and would have died for (ANNIE *makes a gesture of deprecation*) Unnatural child ! no words ; marry, starve, die—anything ! I know you no more !

Annie. What have I done, dear father ?

White. What have you done ? False girl ; deceitful beyond your years—never let me see you—hear of you again !

Annie. Is this because you have learned we love each other ? I couldn't help it, father——

White. Love *him !*—a blight on your love——

Annie. Father, in pity—are you mad ?

White. *Your* work—I am ! Must I force you out ? (*dragging her up the stage, towards* R.) Go to him, go to him ! wait my death ; gloat over the thought, and see what you'll get. Out of my house forever ! (*thrusts her out at door*, R. U. E., *and bolts the door—Music, pianissimo,* (" *Early Love,*") *to the end of Act*

—WHITE *rushes to the table, supporting himself by a chair, and looking round at his desolate apartment till his eye rests on the piano; suddenly he bursts into a flood of tears*) Hated by all the world—I am alone—alone now! (*frantically throwing himself into the chair and dashing his head on the table.*

END OF FIRST ACT.

———

ACT II.

Scene.—*White's Bedroom. An old-fashioned Apartment, but neat and clean. An old easy chair in front,* L., *over the back and arm of which hang White's coat, waistcoat, and necktie.*

The curtain rises to the air of "Early Love" played piano, and through the music, a church clock is heard to strike five. At the end of the strain, WHITE, *who is in the bed, draws aside the curtain next the audience, and looks out.*

White. That must be five o'clock p. m., and I've had nothing to eat since yesterday. I wonder how long I shall last at that little game? It's very lonely here—not a sound stirring; confound those varmints of mice—what a row they're kicking up! Not that I want anybody; I hate the world. (*a knocking as at a door below, is heard*) Ah, knock away! you can't come in till I'm gone aloft. After all, it's a delicious feeling to think one can go out of the world without causing any one to snivel—not even one's——(*glancing up at the picture of* ANNIE) That picture haunts me; I can't look at it, and I can't *help* looking at it—I can't sleep for it—I can't *die* for it! I'll turn it to the wall, I will. (WHITE *who has on his breeches and boots, gets up, and stands on the bed to turn the picture*) This is not a comfortable way of going to bed; but a heart-broken man has no energy to pull off his boots. There, I'm not going to be haunted by you any more. (*turns the portrait face to wall and descends, sitting on the bed*) Poor thing! I wonder where she went to, all night? (*goes to box,* L. *of bed, opens it, and snatches out a paper*) Here it is, here's the policy of insurance; (*coming forward,* C.) here's the magician that tempted my only child to wish me dead, to——(*as he is about to tear it, an old letter drops out*) What's this? (*picks letter up*) Oh, I remember—this is a letter I received five and twenty years ago, giving me an account of my partner—Alick Good's death. (*opens letter and reads it*) "My friend Good, has drowned himself; his last words were, that should you have a child, that child would be the instrument for punishing your crime." The curse is fulfilled—five and twenty year after it was pronounced I *am* punished ; I'll get into bed again. (*throws papers into the box, and jumps into bed*) That's the most comfortable place to enjoy remorse, and a broken heart. (*a tap is heard at the room door*) Hark, there's a rat now ! (*throws a slipper,* L., *and lies down, covering his head with the bed clothes*)

Enter MRS. SADDRIP *at door in flat,* R. C., *with a basket in her hand, and goes to table,* R.; *her back is to* WHITE, *who hearing a sound, starts up, looks around, and suddenly sees her.*

Who's that ? (*she turns round*) Mrs. Saddrip ! how dare you come into my bedroom ? (*drawing the sheet tightly round him*) You once prophesied I should hang myself, didn't you ? You're a witch, a witch ! in the good old times you'd have been horse-ponded ! (*turning from her*) I've read the History of England ; they'd have made it hot for you in Queen Mary's time. (*turns and sees* MRS. SADDRIP *sitting by his bedside—he suddenly drops and draws the clothes over his head*)

Mrs. S. (*sitting,* L. C., *at back*) I've no reason to have any regard for you, that's certain ; but in a civilized country one can't let a fellow creature die for want of a little help. I'm glad to find you've recovered your hearing.

White. Are you ? I'm not ! How did you get in ?

Mrs. S. I got over the rails, and came in the back way.

White. (*sitting up in bed*) Oh, did you ? I'll prosecute you for a trespass.

Mrs. S. Do, if you like. Your shutters have been up all day, and I feared something was wrong with you. (*rising and going to table*) I've brought you some breakfast.

White. I don't want it ! I won't have it—It's pisoned.

Mrs. S. (*fetching little table from* L.) You're a foolish man ; but you must live to be wiser and better—I'll put this little table by your bedside ; there. (*places it*) Now your food on it, and you can reach comfortably.

White. I don't want to reach comfortably ; take it away !

Mrs. S. (*taking things out of her basket, and placing them on table, having first spread a napkin*) There's a cup and saucer.

White. Take 'em away !

Mrs. S. Bread and butter.

White. Take it away !

Mrs. S. An egg.

White. (*pushing it away*) Don't lay your eggs here !

Mrs. S. And there's one of my boys outside with some hot coffee. (*goes to door in flat, where a coffee pot is handed in to her, which she takes, and returning to* L., *side of little table, pours out coffee)* It's all ready, milked and sweetened.

White. I don't want to be sweetened ! Well, of all the impudence—*(solemnly)* Mrs. Saddrip, do you think me such a wretch, that I can eat anything, while, for what I know, my child is starving ? Don't you know I turned her out of my house?

Mrs. S. I do indeed.

White. Do—do you know anything of her ?

Mrs. S. I shall not tell you, till you have taken this cup of coffee. *(forces it on him)*

White. I won't touch it ! *(drinks it)* Now tell me.

Mrs. S. Eat this first. *(offering bread and butter)*

White. *(jumping out of bed)* Woman ! What of my child ?

Mrs. S. *(running to* R.) Bless the man ; he's gone to bed with his boots on !

White. (L. C.) Never mind my boots ;—my child—tell me of her !

Mrs. S. *I* have taken care she should be sheltered.

White. *(grasping her hand)* Bless you for it ! Bless you ! bless you !

Mrs. S. But the poor girl is heart-broken.

White. Heart-broken ?—I am glad of it !—so am I !

Mrs. S. You must let her come back.

White. Never ! never ! never !—till I am gone aloft ;—she shall not want, Mrs. Saddrip, but I couldn't look'on her again. *(bursts into tears)* Oh, Mrs. Saddrip, I'm a wretched man.

Mrs. S. I know you are. *(going up and returning with plate to* R. C.) Take some bread and butter.

White. I shan't ! Oh yes, I know what *you* are ; you think you're getting over me by this tomfoolery, but my executors shall carry my cowshed through your premises for all that. *(goes up towards the bed)*

Mrs. S. (R. C.) And turn me out of my house ; well, I'm not as some poor wretches are—without a friend in the world to give me a good word.

White. *(turning round to her)* Ah, that's what I call a nasty slur ; don't look at me in that insinuating way, Mrs. Saddrip ; I know you hate me. *(throws himself into an arm-chair which stands* L.)

Mrs. S. I don't hate anybody ; nor fear anybody, if it comes to that.

White. *(languidly)* You needn't fear *me ;* I'm not long for this world ; I shall soon go aloft, like poor Thomas Bowling.

Mrs. S. You !—you'll never go aloft, if you behave so cruelly to your daughter who loves you.

White. *She*—love me ? She hates me ! Don't contradict me —I'm " a wicked old fellow, and do nothing but mischief."

Mrs. S. I'm not going to contradict you.

White. (*rising*) She said that I——(*aside*) No, no, poor girl ; it's not for *me* to expose her. (*going up to* R. *of little table*) But Mrs. S., will you do me a favor?

Mrs. S. (L. *of table, handing plate*) If you'll eat some bread and butter ; not without.

White. (*seizing a slice of bread and butter, and eating*) There ; you think you're saving my life by this, don't you ? (*sits and places his hand on his heart*) My disease is here ; bread and butter won't cure *that !*

Mrs. S. Now what's this favor ?

White. You'll have no reason to regret my asking it. Do you know the stationer's at the corner—to the right—number nineteen, you know ? Go there and get me a form of a will ; it will be a shilling—here's the money.

Mrs. S. I've brought one of my lads with me ; he's outside, and will go on that, or any other errand. I shall leave him with you. (*crossing to door in flat,* R.)

White. I'd rather be alone ;—lads, indeed ;—I don't want to be buoyed up in that way.

Mrs. S. Oh, but you must have somebody here, to let us know when you've gone aloft !   **Exit,** *door in flat.*

White. (*hastily putting down the cup which he had raised to his lips*) That's true. Now that woman has a kind heart ; she's not a bad sort ; I thought she was, and I've behaved like a brute to her ; I'll make it up to her (*rises and comes forward* C.) in a way she little expects.

Re-enter MRS. SADDRIP, *at door in flat,* R.

Mrs. S. (*going to chair,* L.) Here, put your things on : you'll get the lumbago, standing about in your shirt sleeves.

White. What's the lumbago to a man in my decomposed state ?

Mrs. S. Stuff ! put on your waistcoat. (*takes it from chair,* L., *and forces it on him*) Now, where's your cravat ?

White. I can die very comfortably without a cravat.

Mrs. S. (*coming round to* R. C.) Here it is ; hold up your head.

White. (C.) Ah, I shall never hold up my head again—never ! MRS. SADDRIP *places her hand under his chin, and raises his head ; and begins tying on his cravat*) Milky White has done with pumps and vanities. (*his eyes rest on her as she is tying a bow*) Mrs. S., you've been a creamy sort of woman in your time, had a good many followers, I dare say ? (MRS. SADDRIP *gets his coat and helps him on with it, standing behind him*—WHITE, C.) By the bye, talking about followers, I should like you to follow me to—what's the name of the place—that celebrated Green ?

Mrs. Sadd. (*putting her head over his right shoulder*) Gretna Green?

White. Gretna devil! (MRS. SADDRIP *goes to dressing table,* R., *for comb and brush, having first placed a chair,* C., *on which* WHITE *sits*) Ken—Kensal Green Cemetery; in fact you're the only one that I know of who would do it.

Mrs S. (R. C.) Your daughter.

White. (*jumping up, excitedly*) Woman! if you name *her* again, I won't answer for the consequences. (MRS. SADDRIP *places her hands on his shoulders and gently forces him back into the chair*) Why do you torture me with——? (*as he attempts to rise, she repeats the action*) Why do——(*he subsides as she soothes him and standing behind, begins combing his hair*) What are you doing,—combing my hair? Stop a minute, Mrs. S., I have it parted on the left side.—I couldn't die comfortably without a proper parting. (*as* MRS. SADDRIP *comes to* R. C.) Mrs. Saddrip, I declare to goodness, I always thought you was carrotty; why you're a——

Mrs. S. (*brushing his hair*) Ha' done!

White. Well, it *would* be a dun in a cow; it's auburn in a woman.

Mrs. S. (*behind him*) How you are going on.

White. Going on? I shall be going off soon—Oh, Mrs. S., don't do that; don't part my hair behind! I look upon that as puppyish.

Mrs. S. Goodness! how bald you're getting at the back.

White. That's right—go it! I knew you'd have something spiteful to say as soon as my back was turned—now, you shan't do it at all; go away. (*rises and goes to the seat in front of the bed and* R. *of the little table; his back towards* R.)

Mrs. S. I can hear the boy at the door. Come in, William. (MRS. SADDRIP *goes to the door in* F., *opens it and* ANNIE *appears with a paper in her hands*)

Mrs. S. (*aside to* ANNIE) *You* here! You should not have come yet.

Annie. (*aside to* MRS. SADDRIP) I must—I must speak to him. (*she sinks into the chair, which is at the head of the bed, and buries her face in her hands*)

White. (*sitting with his back towards them*) What's all that scuffling about? If you've anything to say, why don't you say it out? Is that the boy?

Mrs. S. Yes; he'll go downstairs, and wait there to see if you want anything. (*to* ANNIE *coaxingly*) Won't you dear? (ANNIE *signifies by action that she shall remain*)

White. I hope that's not the atrocious young rascal as used to chevy in my yard and ya-hoo me? Now then, where's the will paper?

Mrs. S. (R. C., *back—taking the paper from* ANNIE *and giving it to* WHITE) Here it is.

White. (*looking at it*) "Where the property is left to a stranger in blood," that's all right. (*opening it out on table*) You'll find pen and ink on the mantel-piece. (MRS. SADDRIP *crosses to* L. *and brings them to him ;* WHITE *waves his hand for her to remove the other things ; she fetches her basket and places the articles in it*) Take away this fodder ; I loathe the sight of food. (MRS. SADDRIP *is removing his bread and butter*) Here, stop ! I'll finish my bread and butter. (*takes it from her and eats*) Now then—in the first place, what's the day of the month ?

Mrs. S. (*standing* L. *of table*) The seventh of October.

White. (*writing*) And what is your Christian name ?

Mrs. S. Martha. (*aside*) What does he want with my name ?

White. Martha Saddrip, you're what we call in the law—a relick, ar'n't you ?

Mrs. S. A relish ?

White. A relish—pooh ! I didn't say "relish." You're a widow, ain't you ?

Mrs. S. That's *my* business ! (*crosses to* R.)

White. (*writing*) All right ; don't be crusty. Now look here, this must be detested by a witness, and then I'll sign it. (*partially turning towards her*) Mrs. Saddrip, I've left you a policy of insurance for four thousand pound, for you have shown kindness to a poor deserted old fellow, whose only child—wishes him out of the world. (*wipes his eyes and turns towards the table*)

Annie. (*at back, scarcely able to restrain her feelings*) Fa——

Mrs S. (*up,* R. C., *aside to her*) Hush ! (*to* WHITE) Soh, this is for me, is it ? (*takes up the will paper and crosses to* L.) Then of course I can do what I like with it, and this is what it deserves. (*tears it up and throws the pieces into the fireplace,* L. 2 E.) I had hope that you were a better man—that your heart was turning ; go aloft indeed ! it's my opinion that a man who forgets his own flesh and blood and carries vindictiveness into the grave is a good way on the road in another direction. (*pointing downwards*)

White. (*loudly blowing his nose, and settling himself in his chair*) Mrs. Saddrip, you found me in a very low state——

Mrs. S. You'll go lower still if——

White. (*jumping up*) Silence, woman ! You've had your turn, haven't you ?—well then, let me have mine. (*sits*) I have no vindictiveness to my child—tell her so. (*emphatically*) Tell her so ! Tell her, that with all her cruel thoughts of *me* I love *her*, still ; but my money would now carry ill luck to her, and degraded as she is by her choice——

Mrs. S. Of a lover you mean to say ? Excuse me, but I consider him a very superior young man, and anybody but you would feel proud of the connection.

White. Mrs. Saddrip, I should be sorry to call you a fool ; but, good gracious, when you tell me to my face that I ought to feel proud of a fellow with no more brains than one of my own cows——

Mrs. S. I wish you had as much ; but there, I'm not going to quarrel with you again. (*crosses to* R.) I'll find some one to look after your cows ; the poor things haven't been milked to-day.

White. Going to leave me all alone ?

Mrs. S. (*behind* WHITE, *placing her hand coaxingly on his shoulder*) May I bring *her* ?

White. (*turning suddenly*) Would you torture me ? No, tell her all here (*placing his hand on his breast*) is grief, not anger *now* ; but don't ask me to see her—oh no ! no ! (*turns, and buries his face in his hands—leaning on table*)

Mrs. S. Well, reflect for a few minutes ; here's some one within call if you think better of it. (*as she passes out at door, with her basket, she endeavors to lead* ANNIE *away, who resists and remains in the same position at the head of the bed*)

White. (*calling after her*) Don't be long, Martha ! (*to himself*) It fills one with dissolving emotions to find there is some one in the world who does care a little for Milky White—just a little—just a little—(*suddenly recollecting and leaning back*) Boy, are you there ?

Annie. I'm here, sir !

White. You're not the boy as threw a dead rat into my water butt, are you ?

Annie. (*at back*) Oh, no, sir.

White. Lucky for you. I say, what do the boys say of me in the neighborhood ; they all hate Milky White, don't they ? I don't wonder if they do ; I made myself a bugbear to everybody —I was wicked enough to love only one—and she—even my daughter, hated,—despised me !

Annie. Oh, no ! no ! (*sobs*)

White. Why, what are you blubbering about ? What a soft-hearted, soft-headed boy you must be ; *I've* more reason to cry than you have, and I'm as dry as a bone. (*wiping his eyes*)

Annie. Your daughter always loved—does love you !

White. Oh no, no, no ! My eyes showed me a glittering coin; at last, I heard it sounded—'twas base ! 'twas base !

Annie. Don't—don't say that !

White. That voice ! (WHITE *rises and turns towards* ANNIE) Ah, she, *she !* Mercy on me ; my Annie. (*throws himself into chair, as* ANNIE *advances, and falls at his feet,* R. C.)

Annie. Father ! Don't turn me from you again. (*takes his hand, which* WHITE *snatches from her*)

White. (*turning his face from* ANNIE, *and waving her away with his right hand*) Go, go, go !

Annie. (*earnestly, and with difficulty suppressing her sobs*) If I have hurt you by unwisely accepting the affection of another, I renounce it ! Do you think I have forgotten all your tenderness to me ? Don't accuse me of not loving you, father ; for years I have never laid my head on my pillow without a prayer for you.

White. A blight on the man who gave me back my hearing !

Annie. (*sadly*) He will never come again. Don't father— don't be harsher with me than I can bear ; these words are so new to me ; they kill me ! (*falls with her head on his knee*)

White. (*looking round on her—aside*) After all, how could I expect a child to love one so hated as I have been. (*to her—gently*) Annie ! Annie !—my—my child, come here. (*rises and leads her forward* C.) Tell me—do you think you could learn to love me—even now, if I tried to live to do good, if I——

Annie. (R. C.) I couldn't love you more than I have done, father.

White. Ah, don't say that, don't say that ! After being dead to sound for nine weary years, I could have taken back my afflictions, with gratitude, if the first thing I heard had also been the last—your song ! (*in a burst of feeling*) If I could only have a dream of the joy I felt at hearing those words ! (*to* ANNIE) Sing it again, my girl ; if anything could make me forget your— cruel confession—it's that !

Annie. I will sing it, father, though I could rather cry, at hearing you ask it so sadly.

(WHITE *turns from her, and as she sings displays great emotion—and gradually turns his face towards her*)

Annie.   Whom did I love as time flew on,
And she was lost—forever gone ?
Whose doting lip was ever near,
To kiss away my orphan tear ?
Whose fond affection taught me then,
With ardor fresh to love again ?
No stranger lur'd my heart ; but rather
I clung alone to thee—my——

(ANNIE *unable to proceed, bursts into tears;* WHITE *snatches her to his heart, tenderly embracing her*)

White. Annie—my child—if I had heard no more than that——

Annie. I don't understand you——

White. You shall have all when I am gone, my girl, *you shall!* but don't say you wish me dead !

Annie. Oh, father !

White. Where did you stay last night ?

Annie. Next door ; Mrs. Saddrip was as kind to me as a mother could have been.

White. Mrs. Saddrip ! she's a woman, in the most embracing sense of the word. I can hear her coming—go just now ; but come back ; be a good girl, and I'll try to forget what I heard— I will—I will.

Goes up, C.; ANNIE *goes towards the door, then turns, rushes into* WHITE'S *arms, kisses him affectionately, and* **exit,** *door in flat.*

Enter MRS. SADDRIP, *door in flat.*

Mrs. S. (*at door, shaking her finger at* WHITE, *who stands* L. C.) What, have you been ill-using that poor, motherless girl again ?

White. (*shaking his finger at* MRS. SADDRIP) Mrs. Saddrip ; you're an artful, good-hearted, meddling woman, that's what you are. (*goes forward,* L. C., MRS. SADDRIP, R. C.) Make your mind perfectly easy ; she shall be my child again, and I'll try to do a little good before I go aloft.

'**Mrs. S.** (R. C.) Ah ! then you may stand a chance of an up-ward movement.

White. Mrs. Saddrip, you once went so far as to say my wife never loved me,—you were right. I made her believe that her lover—my partner, had deserted her. She married me out of revenge to him.

Mrs. S. You shocking man !

White. Ain't I ?—an out-and-outer. The poor weak-minded fellow, Alick Good, went and destroyed himself in a fit of trum-pery insanity.

Mrs. S. And all through you ?

White. That's a comfortable thing to have on one's con-science to go aloft with, isn't it ?

Mrs. S. Oh, you men—you men—you're all a bad lot !

White. I thought the same of women once ; but Mrs. S., I now look upon *you* as an angel.

Mrs. S. A middle-aged one.

White. You must help me to do the right thing.

Mrs. S. Your daughter——

White. She'll have some other object—perhaps any quantity of little objects to attend to—she'll marry.

Mrs. S. Perhaps not.

White. Oh, yes, she must—she must ; I never denied her a toy in my life. If she has fixed her mind upon a husband, she shall have it ; though I wish—yes, I do wish she had had better taste. (*going up*) You must take pity on a poor deserted fellow——

Mrs. S. (R. C.) What, when you mean to have me turned out of my house—perhaps to ruin me ?

White. Nothing further from my thoughts ; in fact, if you'd given me time, I might have finished a long conversation by making a honorable proposal ; the idea had just struck me that I might carry out my good designs and my cowshed at the same time. (*hands a chair to* MRS. SADDRIP, *who sits*, R. C.) My bump of benevolence is springing up like a toad-stool—I mean, a mushroom ; don't you be the one to trample on it. (*sits beside her*, L. C.)

Mrs. S. Oh, Mr. White——

White. Take me in hand ; I'll be a father to your boys, even to the atrocious young rascal who ya-hoo'd me. I'll love everybody.

Mrs. S. Mr. White, you force me to disclose a sad secret—I am *not* a widow !

White. Not a widow ? (*rising, and drawing his chair away from her*) In the name of all that's respectable, what are you then ?

Mrs. S. A wife.

White. (*dropping into his chair*) Milky White's knocked over again. Who is your good man ?

Mrs. S. A bad man—very much older than myself, who deserted me just before the birth of my second boy——

White. The ya-hoo ?

Mrs. S. And though he has the means, he has never done anything to assist me, and I had too much pride ever to compel it.

White. (*aside*) And I have persecuted this poor creature. (*to her*) Mrs. S., all I can say is, the sooner your brute of a husband goes aloft the better ; perhaps you'll come in for something then.

Mrs. S. No, his property goes to a younger brother, a spendthrift, who has, I hear, already sold his expectations.

White. Ah, you've shown me that crushing troubles may be borne with a countenance all serene : and I'll try and make the best of mine if you'll find that boy Dick, and send him to me.

Mrs. S. (*rising and going to door in flat*) He's in the yard, milking the cows ; I persuaded him to do that for you, and really he's not a bad-hearted lad.

White. (*still seated*, L. C.) Well, that's about all one can say for him. (*exit* MRS. SADDRIP, *door in flat*) Poor soul ! poor soul ! Why can't people exercise the organ of benevolence ? look at me ! see what good *I* do—I mean, what good I *mean* to do ; my darling will not wish me dead then. (*a tap is heard at door in flat*) Come in, whoever you are.

The door opens and DICK *appears, timidly putting his head in.*

White. (*aside*) Well, however she could hang her affections on a peg like that, gets over me. (*rises*) However, it's done! what's done can't be undone! (*aloud to* DICK, *and approaching him*) Come in my—my—fine fellow! (DICK *hesitates*) Don't be frightened—be a man. (C. *at back*) I behaved rather roughly to you yesterday.

Dick. (*looking at his throat in looking-glass on table,* R.) You only strangled me; I'm black and blue.

White. You do look blue. Well, my lad, I'm sorry for it.

Dick. (*aside* R., *astonished*) Laws! he can hear!

White. Now that's the first time you ever heard Milky White say such a thing as that, isn't it?

Dick. The most onnatural thing from you as I ever did hear.

White. (*placing a chair,* R. C.) Sit down here beside me.

Dick. (*receding up,* R.) Now look'ee, master—none o' your tricks. I know your game, if I set down there, you'll jump up and burke me.

White. No, Dick, I'm changed; my bump has come out within the last hour.

Dick. What bump?

White. (*petulantly*) Sit down! The bump of benevolence.

Dick. (*aside* R.) "Sit down on my bump of benevolence!" —he's cracked. (*draws the chair away from* WHITE, *who has seated himself* C., *and timidly sits on the edge.*)

White. (*aside*) Did any one ever see such an ill-bred calf? (*aloud to* DICK) Look here, if you sit on a chair like that, you'll cut yourself. (*draws nearer to* DICK, *who exhibits apprehension*) You proposed yesterday that I should give you a third of the business.

Dick. Yes, and you guv me a kick instead.

White. (*rising*) You shall have it now.

Dick. (*rising and retreating to* R.—*alarmed*) What, a kick?

White. No, no, a third of the bus—don't look such an ass, there's a good fellow!—a third of the business; do your best in it; it will all be yours, when I am gone aloft. (*reseats himself,* C.)

Dick. Are you chaffing me, governor? (*sits again,* R. C.)

White. No; I mean it. I only ask you one thing; don't— don't teach my child to think I live too long.

Dick. (*aside*) I think he's got the delirium tremendous.

White. And be you kind to her; she has risked everything for you.

Dick. Have she though? What have she risked?

White. No matter; you had told my child that you loved her, had you not? (DICK *scratches his head*) Don't scratch your head, but answer "yes" or "no."

Dick. Yes, I sartinly did wunst ; but she's guvven me turnups.

White. So she told me ; but I see she can't be happy with anybody else, she shall be——(*as* WHITE *is about to place his hand on* DICK'S *shoulder,* DICK *again retreats into* R. *corner* —WHITE *turns from him with ineffable disgust—aside*) Upon my soul, this fellow makes me quite sick ! (*to him, with an effort*) She shall be yours. (*aside*) My bump of benevolence must be swelling up like a young balloon. (*going up,* C.)

Dick. (R.) Good gracious ! you've took away my breath.

White. Yes, but don't look such an ass.

Dick. Well, but stop—afore we go any further—(*following* WHITE *up* C.) how about her tale of the four thousand pound, and——

White. (*turning upon him furiously*) Selfish idiot ! (DICK *runs back to* R.) Say no more about *that* if you're wise—you fool ! Don't you see I wish to be benevolent if I can ?

Dick. (*aside,* R.) Oh, I see ; she only told me the tale about the doctor chap to teaze me—she's like all the gals. (*to* WHITE) Guv'nor, you've guv me a hoister up, and no mistake : half an hour ago I was kicking the cows out of vexation ; now I could kiss 'em all round out of delightfulness. Bless her pretty eyes— won't I just love her—and you, too, father-in-law ! (*crossing,* L. *to* WHITE, *who retreats to* R., *back*)

White. (*at back*) Father-in-law ! (*aside*) Ugh ! that's a dose.

Enter ANNIE, D. *in flat* (*not seeing* WHITE).

Annie. (*coming down,* R. C.) Ah, Dick, I'm glad indeed to see *you* here ; are you friends with my father ?

Dick. (L. C.) Friends ! we're going to be blood relations by marriage. Oh, you pussy cat ! haven't you been a playing with my feelings !

White. (*coming between them,* C.) Silence'! let *me* speak. Annie, my girl, I'll give you the hardest proof that any one could have asked of me, that my love can deny you nothing. Kiss me first.

Annie. (*kisses him*) Do I not know that ?

White. (*to* ANNIE—*and pointing to* DICK) There—take it ! take it ! No matter what I could have wished—take it !

Annie. (R. C.) What do you mean, father ?

Dick. (L.) He means what he says ; I thought at fust he didn't—but he do. Come on ! (*extending his arms*)

White. (C.) It—I mean that boy, windmill—or whatever it is—shall be your husband.

Annie. Oh, father !

Dick. Come on ; it's all right.

Annie. You don't mean to force me to such a union ?

White. Force you! (*bitterly*) You have forced *me*, child.

Dick. My *partener* here, seeing as we love each other, consents to the match like a brick : come on !

White. (*watching* ANNIE'S *countenance*) Do you *not* love him ?

Annie. Oh, no ! no ! no !

White. (*clasping his hands in rapture*) Thank mercy ! thank mercy ! (*to* DICK) Stand out of the way ! (*pushes* DICK *roughly—*DICK *falls into arm chair,* L.) Is it true ? (*goes up* C., *embracing* ANNIE)

Dick. What are you going on like that for ? What d'ye both mean ? (*crying*) What are you making a April fool of a poor lad for ? I never did *you* no harm. (*goes up to the bed and sits on it, blubbering*)

Enter MRS. SADDRIP, door in flat.

Mrs S. (*up,* C.) Neighbor White, here's——

White. Stop ! stop ! that fellow's making a pocket-handkerchief of my counterpane. (*crosses to* DICK) Get up ! DICK *moves, and sits on the box at the foot of the bed—to* MRS. SADDRIP) I beg your pardon ; go on.

Mrs. S. Here's a young gentleman outside the door wishes to be reconciled to you again ; I have promised to speak for him.

White. (L. C.) She cow-doctor ? Trot him in ! let him look at my bump of benevolence to-day.

MRS. SADDRIP beckons ARCHIBALD, who enters at door in flat and comes down, R. C.

White. (C.) Well, young Smith, and what have you to say ?

Arch. (R. C.) This, sir, that notwithstanding your severe treatment of me, because I entertained an affection for your daughter——

White. (*astonished*) You entertained an affection ! What are you talking about ?

Arch. Inasmuch as you are her father, I will relieve your mind of a weight, which it has borne long enough. My name is not Smith but Good.

White. Good——

Annie. (L.) Gracious !

Arch. The son of your former partner, who you thought had destroyed himself ; the fact is, he has been dead only two years.

White. Boy, boy ! you're lifting me from a mattress of thorns to a feather bed ; swear it's true !

Arch. I do.

White. And you love my child.

Arch. Tenderly.

White. And she returns it ?

Arch. Ask her.

Dick. (*at back*) Oh, she'll say anything.

White. (*who has crossed to* R. C., *turns to* DICK) Lie down ! (*to* ANNIE, *taking her hand, and pointing to* ARCHIBALD, *who is* C.) Annie, my girl, is this the man you loved !

Annie. (R., *casting her eyes down*) Yes, dear father.

Dick. (*at back*) Oh, shame ! shame !

White. (*flinging hair brush at* DICK) I'll shame you ! Get out !

Arch. You knew me to be poor, and that prevented me from making known to you my hopes, but I had told Annie that I held a reversion to four thousand pounds on the death of an old fellow ; I have just heard that he is dead, consequently I am no longer penniless.

White. (*in a tone of deep remorse*) Oh, Annie, my girl—my girl—can you forgive me ?

Annie. Forgive you ?

White. Ah, yes ; when that scientific young cow-doctor had given me back the blessing of hearing, I heard you say something to Dick about your expectations of a bad man's death; of course I thought you meant your father—oh fool ! fool !

Dick. (*at back*) Oh, fool ! fool !

White. (*to* DICK) How dare you to call *me* a fool *Me* a fool, you hass !

Arch. And you thought I'd divulged your assurance secret ? oh, that accounts for my being turned out.

Dick. (*coming down*, L. C.) Turned out, I was kicked out ! in a most undelicate way too.

White. What unbelieving monster has been turning that picture ? (*jumps on the bed and re-turns picture, and points to* DICK) You did that ; I saw you do it. (*comes* R. C. *between* ANNIE *and* ARCHIBALD) Take her ! I shall lose my child, but I shall get a son-in-law I'm proud of. (*crosses to* C., *and goes up, pointing to* DICK) I couldn't stomach *it!* (WHITE *goes up to* MRS. SADDRIP.)

Dick. (L.) It ? What are you it-ting me for ? (*aside*) I suppose I'm to stick to a third of the business.

Arch. (R. C., *to* ANNIE, R.) On we go to happiness ! Annie, you shall be the wife of a great ear-doctor ; I can afford to pursue my studies with the money I get by John Saddrip's death, and——

Mrs. S. (*up*, L. C.) Ah ! (*appears to be fainting ;* WHITE *supports her.*)

White. (*up*, C.) My dear soul, what is the matter ?

Mrs S. (*coming down*, L. C.) John—John Saddrip !

White. (C., *aside to her*) Oh, I see—I see ! .

Mrs. S. (*to* ARCHIBALD) Was he living at Cricklewood ?

White. (*hurriedly*) Washecrickleivingwood ?

Arch. (R. C.) Just so.

White. (*delighted, and aside to* MRS. SADDRIP) It's all right ; the brute's gone aloft ! you are a widow—you *are* a relish now. (*to others*) This lady knew the party as is departed, and according to all accounts he was a party who had *not* the bump of benevolence, eh, doctor ?

Arch. And consequently was only an incumbrance on the earth. (*goes up the stage with* ANNIE.)

White. Not like us, eh, Mrs. S. !—Widow S. ! Will you allow me to whisper, Widow S. ? (WHITE *whispers in her ear,* MRS. SADDRIP *in return whispers something in* WHITE'S *ear, at which he exhibits delight—business repeated* ad libitum) Exactly—of course—delicacy ; yes, yes ; when a proper time has elapsed. I shall be the happiest, gayest-hearted dairyman alive. (*to* DICK *who is sitting, the picture of despair, in the arm-chair,* L.) Oh ! (*pointing at him*) A sick monkey. (*aloud to* DICK) Holloa, boy ! don't look so glum ; you shall be my foreman and cowkeeper extraordinary. (*turns to* ARCHIBALD) Here, cowdoctor ; just look at my organ of benevolence now ; I mean to go the whole lump I can tell you. (ANNIE *crosses to him,* R. C.) I love my child as much as ever I did, for she's a dear good girl ; but (*turning to* MRS. SADDRIP, *who is* L. C.) here's a dear good woman, who has taught me, that in passing through this subloonary milk-walk, we ought to have a kind word for all our fellow-creatures ; let us be deaf only to the voice of selfishness—let us return good for evil—and a light heart will be our reward. Only to think what a grim black-hearted bogie *I* was. (ANNIE *and* MRS. SADDRIP *approach him expostulating*). Yes, I was Annie,—yes, I was, Martha ; but now with benevolence for my motto, my hope shall be to merit approbation when my character appears " MILKY WHITE."

ARCHIBALD. ANNIE. WHITE. MRS. SADDRIP. DICK.

R. C. L.

CURTAIN.

EARLY LOVE.

1. Whom did I love, when on her breast I

hour - ly sought my infant rest, Whom did I trust in

ere my tongue could mock the lul-la - by she sung? Whose

gentle form, whose watching eye, In cra-dle dream seem'd ev - er

nigh; I had not learn'd to know an-o-ther, For

then I on-ly lov'd my moth-er.

UNCLE TOM'S CABIN (NEW VERSION.)

A MELODRAMA IN FIVE ACTS, BY CHAS. TOWNSEND.

PRICE, 15 CENTS.

Seven male, five female characters (some of the characters play two parts). Time of playing, 2¼ hours. This is a new acting edition of a prime old favorite, so simplified in the stage-setting as to be easily represented by dramatic clubs and travelling companies with limited scenery. UNCLE TOM'S CABIN is a play that never grows old ; being pure and faultless, it commands the praise of the pulpit and support of the press, while it enlists the favor of all Christians and heads of families. It will draw hundreds where other plays draw dozens, and therefore is sure to fill any hall.

SYNOPSIS OF INCIDENTS: ACT I.—*Scene I.*—The Shelby plantation in Kentucky.—George and Eliza.—The curse of Slavery.—The resolve.—Off for Canada.—" I won't be taken—I'll die first."—Shelby and Haley.—Uncle Tom and Harry must be sold.—The poor mother.—" Sell my boy!"—The faithful slave. *Scene II.*—Gumption Cute.—" By Gum!"—Marks, the lawyer.—A mad Yankee.—George in disguise.—A friend in need.—The human bloodhounds.—The escape.—" Hooray fer old Varmount ! "

ACT II.—St. Clare's elegant home.—The fretful wife.—The arrival.—Little Eva.—Aunt Ophelia and Topsy.—" O, Golly ! I'se so wicked !"—St. Clare's opinion.—" Benighted innocence."—The stolen gloves.—Topsy in her glory.

ACT III.—The angel child.—Tom and St. Clare.—Topsy's mischief.—Eva's request.—The promise.—pathetic scene.—Death of Eva.—St. Clare's grief.—" For thou art gone forever."

ACT IV.—The lonely house.—Tom and St. Clare.—Topsy's keepsake.—Deacon Perry and Aunt Ophelia.—Cute on deck.—A distant relative.—The hungry visitor.—Chuck full of emptiness."—Cute and the Deacon.—A row.—A fight.—Topsy to the rescue.—St. Clare wounded.— Death of St. Clare.—" Eva—Eva—I am coming "

ACT V.—Legree's plantation on the Red River.—Home again.—Uncle Tom's noble heart.—" My soul ain't yours, Mas'r."—Legree's cruel work.—Legree and Cassy.—The white slave.—A frightened brute.—Legree's fear.—A life of sin.—Marks and Cute.—A new scheme.—The dreadful whipping of Uncle Tom.—Legree punished at last.—Death of Uncle Tom.—Eva in Heaven.

THE WOVEN WEB.

A DRAMA IN FOUR ACTS, BY CHAS. TOWNSEND.

PRICE, 15 CENTS.

Seven male, three female characters, viz. : leading and second juvenile men, society villain, walking gentleman, eccentric comedian, old man, low comedian, leading juvenile lady, soubrette and old woman. Time of playing, 2¼ hours. THE WOVEN WEB is a flawless drama, pure in thought and action, with excellent characters, and presenting no difficulties in costumes or scenery. The story is captivating, with a plot of the most intense and unflagging interest, rising to a natural climax of wonderful power. The wit is bright and sparkling, the action terse, sharp and rapid. In touching the great chord of human sympathy, the author has expended that rare skill which has given life to every great play known to the stage. This play has been produced under the author's management with marked success, and will prove an unquestionable attraction wherever presented.

SYNOPSIS OF INCIDENTS: ACT I.—Parkhurst & Manning's law office, New York.—Tim's opinion.—The young lawyer.—" Majah Billy Toby, sah!"—Love and law.—Bright prospects.—Bertha's misfortune.—A false friend.—The will destroyed.—A cunning plot.—Weaving the web.—The unseen witness.—The letter.—Accused.—Dishonored.

ACT II.—Winter quarters.—Colonel Hastings and Sergeant Tim.—Moses.—A message.—Tim on his dignity.—The arrival.—Playing soldier.—The secret.—The promise.—Harry in danger.—Love and duty.—The promise kept.—" Saved, at the loss of my own honor!"

ACT III.—Drawing-room at Falconer's.—Reading the news.—"Apply to Judy!"—Louise's romance.—Important news.—Bertha's fears.—Leamington's arrival.—Drawing the web.—Threatened.—Plotting.—Harry and Bertha.—A fiendish lie.—Face to face.—" Do you know him ? "—Denounced.—" Your life shall be the penalty !"—Startling tableau.

ACT IV.—At Uncle Toby's.—A wonderful climate.—An impudent rascal.— A bit of history.—Woman's wit.—Toby Indignant.—A quarrel.—Uncle Toby's evidence.—Leamington's last trump.—Good news.—Checkmated.—The telegram.—Breaking the web.—Sunshine at last.

☞ *Copies mailed, postpaid, to any address, on receipt of the annexed prices.* ☜

SAVED FROM THE WRECK.

A DRAMA IN THREE ACTS, BY THOMAS K. SERRANO.

PRICE, 15 CENTS.

Eight male, three female characters: Leading comedy, juvenile man, genteel villain, rough villain, light comedy, escaped convict, detective, utility, juvenile lady, leading comedy lady and old woman. Two interior and one landscape scenes. Modern costumes. Time of playing, two hours and a half. The scene of the action is laid on the New Jersey coast. The plot is of absorbing interest, the "business" effective, and the ingenious contrasts of comic and serious situations present a continuous series of surprises for the spectators, whose interest is increasingly maintained up to the final tableau.

SYNOPSIS OF INCIDENTS.

ACT I. THE HOME OF THE LIGHT-HOUSE KEEPER.—An autumn afternoon.— The insult.—True to herself.—A fearless heart.—The unwelcome guest.—Only a foundling.—An abuse of confidence.—The new partner.—The compact.—The dead brought to life.—Saved from the wreck.—Legal advice.—Married for money.—A golden chance.—The intercepted letter.—A vision of wealth.—The forgery.—Within an inch of his life.—The rescue.—TABLEAU.

ACT II. SCENE AS BEFORE; time, night.—Dark clouds gathering.—Changing the jackets.—Father and son.—On duty.—A struggle for fortune.—Loved for himself. —The divided greenbacks.—The agreement.—An unhappy life.—The detective's mistake.—Arrested.—Mistaken identity.—The likeness again.—On the right track —The accident.—" Will she be saved ? "—Latour's bravery.—A noble sacrifice.—The secret meeting.—Another case of mistaken identity.—The murder.—" Who did it ? "—The torn cuff.—" There stands the murderer !"—" 'Tis false ! "—The wrong man murdered.—Who was the victim ?—TABLEAU.

ACT III. TWO DAYS LATER.—Plot and counterplot.—Gentleman and convict.— The price of her life.—Some new documents.—The divided banknotes.—Sunshine through the clouds.—Prepared for a watery grave—Deadly peril.—Father and daughter.—The rising tide.—A life for a signature.—True unto death.—Saved.—The mystery solved.—Dénouement.—TABLEAU.

BETWEEN TWO FIRES.

A COMEDY-DRAMA IN THREE ACTS, BY THOMAS K. SERRANO.

PRICE, 15 CENTS.

Eight male, three female, and utility characters: Leading juvenile man, first and second walking gentleman, two light comedians (lawyer and foreign adventurer), Dutch and Irish character comedians, villain, soldiers ; leading juvenile lady, walking lady and comedienne. Three interior scenes ; modern and military costumes. Time of playing, two hours and a half. Apart from unusual interest of plot and skill of construction, the play affords an opportunity of representing the progress of a real battle in the distance (though this is not necessary to the action). The comedy business is delicious, if well worked up, and a startling phase of the slavery question is sprung upon the audience in the last act.

SYNOPSIS OF INCIDENTS.

ACT I. AT FORT LEE, ON THE HUDSON.—News from the war.—The meeting. —The colonel's strange romance.—Departing for the war.—The intrusted packet.—An honest man.—A last request.—Bitter hatred.—The dawn of love.—A northerner's sympathy for the South.—Is he a traitor ?—Held in trust.—La Creole mine for sale.— Financial agents.—A brother's wrong.—An order to cross the enemy's lines.—Fortune's fool.—Love's penalty.—Man's independence.—Strange disclosures.—A shadowed life.—Beggared in pocket, and bankrupt in love.—His last chance.—The refusal.—Turned from home.—Alone, without a name —Off to the war.—TABLEAU.

ACT II. ON THE BATTLEFIELD.—An Irishman's philosophy.—Unconscious of danger.—Spies in the camp.—The insult.—Risen from the ranks.—The colonel's prejudice.—Letters from home.—The plot to ruin.—A token of love.—True to him.— The plotters at work.—Breaking the seals.—The meeting of husband and wife.—A forlorn hope.—Doomed as a spy.—A struggle for lost honor.—A soldier's death.— TABLEAU.

ACT III. BEFORE RICHMOND.—The home of Mrs. De Mori.—The two documents.—A little misunderstanding.—A deserted wife.—The truth revealed.—Brought to light.—Mother and child.—Rowena's sacrifice.—The American Eagle spreads his wings.—The spider's web.—True to himself.—The reconciliation.—A long divided home reunited.—The close of the war.—TABLEAU.

☞ *Copies mailed, postpaid, to any address, on receipt of the annexed prices.* ☜

NEW ENTERTAINMENTS.

THE JAPANESE WEDDING.

A costume pantomime representation of the Wedding Ceremony in Japanese high life. The company consists of the bride and groom, their parents, six bridesmaids, and the officiating personage appropriately called the "Go-between." There are various formalities, including salaams, tea-drinking, eating rice-cakes, and giving presents. No words are spoken. The ceremony (which occupies about 50 minutes), with the "tea-room," fills out an evening well, though music and other attractions may be added. Can be represented by young ladies alone, if preferred. **Price, 25 Cents.**

AN EVENING WITH PICKWICK.

A Literary and Dramatic Dickens Entertainment.—Introduces the Pickwick Club, the Wardles of Dingley Dell, the Fat Boy, Alfred Jingle, Mrs. Leo Hunter, Lord Mutanhed and Count Smorltork, Arabella Allen and Bob Allen, Bob Sawyer, Mrs. and Master Bardell, Mrs. Cluppins, Mrs. Weller, Stiggins, Tony Weller, Sam Weller, and the Lady Traveller. **Price, 25 cents.**

AN EVENING WITH COPPERFIELD.

A Literary and Dramatic Dickens Entertainment.—Introduces Mrs. Copperfield, Davie, the Peggotys, the Murdstones, Mrs. Gummidge, Little Em'ly, Barkis, Betsey Trotwood, Mr. Dick and his kite, Steerforth, the Creakles, Traddles, Rosa Dartle, Miss Mowcher, Uriah Heep and his Mother, the Micawbers, Dora and Gyp, and the wooden-legged Gatekeeper. **Price, 25 cents.**

These "Evenings with Dickens" can be represented in whole or in part, require but little memorizing, do not demand experienced actors, are not troublesome to prepare, and are suitable for performance either on the platform or in the drawing room.

THE GYPSIES' FESTIVAL.

A Musical Entertainment for Young People. Introduces the Gypsy Queen, Fortune Teller, Yankee Peddler, and a Chorus of Gypsies, of any desired number. The scene is supposed to be a Gypsy Camp. The costumes are very pretty, but simple; the dialogue bright; the music easy and tuneful; and the drill movements and calisthenics are graceful. Few properties and no set scenery required, so that the entertainment can be represented on any platform. **Price, 25 cents.**

THE COURT OF KING CHRISTMAS.

A CHRISTMAS ENTERTAINMENT. The action takes place in Santa Claus land on Christmas eve, and represents the bustling preparations of St. Nick and his attendant worthies for the gratification of all children the next day. The cast may include as many as 36 characters, though fewer will answer, and the entertainment represented on a platform, without troublesome properties. The costumes are simple, the incidental music and drill movements graceful and easily managed, the dialogue uncommonly good, and the whole thing quite above the average. A representation of this entertainment will cause the young folks, from six to sixty, fairly to turn themselves inside out with delight, and, at the same time, enforce the important moral of Peace and Good Will. **Price, 25 cents.**

RECENTLY PUBLISHED.

ILLUSTRATED TABLEAUX FOR AMATEURS. A new series of *Tableaux Vivants*, by MARTHA C. WELD. In this series each description is accompanied with a full-page illustration of the scene to be represented.
PART I.—MISCELLANEOUS TABLEAUX.—Contains General Introduction, 12 Tableaux and 14 Illustrations. **Price, 25 Cents.**
PART II.—MISCELLANEOUS TABLEAUX.—Contains Introduction, 12 Tableaux and 12 illustrations. **Price, 25 Cents.**
SAVED FROM THE WRECK. A drama in three acts. Eight male, three female characters. Time, two hours and a half. **Price, 15 Cents.**
BETWEEN TWO FIRES. A comedy-drama in three acts. Eight male, three female characters. Time, two hours and a half. **Price, 15 Cents.**
BY FORCE OF IMPULSE. A drama in five acts. Nine male, three female characters. Time, two hours and a half. **Price, 15 Cents.**
A LESSON IN ELEGANCE. A comedy in one act. Four female characters. Time, thirty minutes. **Price, 15 Cents.**
WANTED, A CONFIDENTIAL CLERK. A farce in one act. Six male characters. Time, thirty minutes. **Price, 15 Cents.**
SECOND SIGHT. A farcical comedy in one act. Four male, one female character. Time, one hour. **Price, 15 Cents.**
THE TRIPLE WEDDING. A drama in three acts. Four male, four female characters. Time, one hour and a quarter. **Price, 15 cents.**

☞ *Any of the above will be sent by mail, postpaid, to any address, on receipt of the annexed prices.* ☜

HAROLD ROORBACH, Publisher, 9 Murray St., New York.

HELMEI
ACTOR'S MAKE

A Practical and Systematic Guide to the Art of Making up for the Stage.

PRICE, 25 CENTS.

WITH EXHAUSTIVE TREATMENT ON THE USE OF THEATRICAL WIGS AND BEARDS, THE MAKE-UP AND ITS REQUISITE MATERIALS, THE DIFFERENT FEATURES AND THEIR MANAGEMENT, TYPICAL CHARACTER MASKS, ETC. WITH SPECIAL HINTS TO LADIES. DESIGNED FOR THE USE OF ACTORS AND AMATEURS, AND FOR BOTH LADIES AND GENTLEMEN. COPIOUSLY ILLUSTRATED.

CONTENTS.

I. THEATRICAL WIGS.—The Style and Form of Theatrical Wigs and Beards. The Color and Shading of Theatrical Wigs and Beards. Directions for Measuring the Head. To put on a Wig properly.

II. THEATRICAL BEARDS.—How to fashion a Beard out of crêpé hair. How to make Beards of Wool. The growth of Beard simulated.

III. THE MAKE-UP.—A successful Character Mask, and how to make it. Perspiration during performance, how removed.

IV. THE MAKE-UP BOX.—Grease Paints. Grease paints in sticks; Flesh Cream; Face Powder; How to use face powder as a liquid cream; The various shades of face powder. Water Cosmétique. Nose Putty. Court Plaster. Cocoa Butter. Crêpé Hair and Prepared Wool. Grenadine. Dorin's Rouge. "Old Man's" Rouge. "Juvenile" Rouge. Spirit Gum. Email Noir. Bear's Grease. Eyebrow Pencils. Artist's Stomps. Powder Puffs. Hares' Feet. Camels'-hair Brushes.

V. THE FEATURES AND THEIR TREATMENT.—The Eyes: blindness. The Eyelids. The Eyebrows: How to paint out an eyebrow or moustache; How to paste on eyebrows; How to regulate bushy eyebrows. The Eyelashes: To alter the appearance of the eyes. The Ears. The Nose: A Roman nose; How to use the nose putty; A pug nose; An African nose; a large nose apparently reduced in size. The Mouth and Lips: a juvenile mouth; an old mouth; a sensuous mouth; a satirical mouth; a one-sided mouth; a merry mouth; A sullen mouth. The Teeth. The Neck, Arms, Hands and Fingernails: Fingernails lengthened. Wrinkles: Friendliness and Sullenness indicated by wrinkles. Shading. A Starving character. A Cut in the Face. A Thin Face Made Fleshy.

VI. TYPICAL CHARACTER MASKS.—The Make-up for Youth: Dimpled cheeks. Manhood. Middle Age. Making up as a Drunkard: One method; another method. Old Age. Negroes. Moors. Chinese. King Lear. Shylock. Macbeth. Richelieu. Statuary. Clowns.

VII. SPECIAL HINTS to LADIES.—The Make-up. Theatrical Wigs and Hair Goods.

Sent by mail, postpaid, to any address, on receipt of the price.

HAROLD ROORBACH, Publisher,
9 Murray Street, New York.